DRAT That Fat Cat!

Julia Patton

ALBERT WHITMAN & COMPANY
CHICAGO, ILLINOIS

MAIL

PUSH

knock
knock

To Mr. & Mrs. Bear and their FAT CAT
—with much love JP

Library of Congress Cataloging-in-Publication
data is on file with the publisher.

Text and pictures copyright © 2016 by Julia Patton
Published in 2016 by Albert Whitman & Company
ISBN 978-0-8075-1713-0

Printed in China
10 9 8 7 6 5 4 3 2 1 LP 25 24 23 22 21 20 19 18 17 16

Design by Jordan Kost

For more information about Albert Whitman & Company,
visit our web site at www.albertwhitman.com.

Cornelius Van Ploof lived alone.

He collected very rare species of cacti.
He disliked noise and mess.

One Sunday morning, there was a

DiNG
DONG!
meeoow!

at the front door.

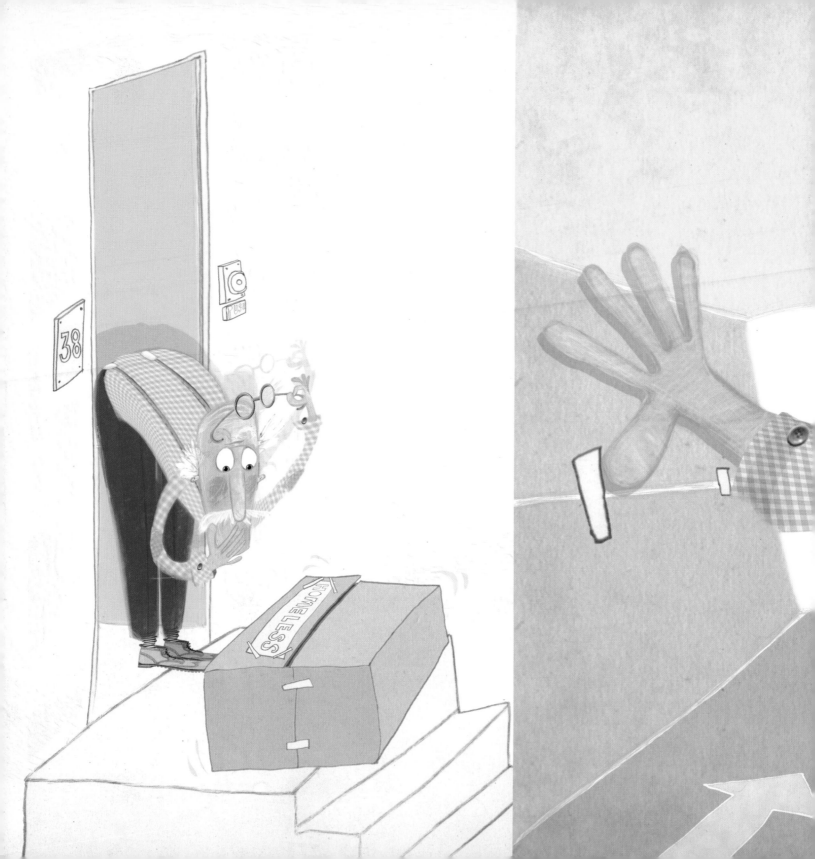

He found a large box, so he carefully opened it to see what was inside.

A furry little paw greeted Cornelius.

Without warning, out jumped a big fat cat who trotted right past him and into the house!

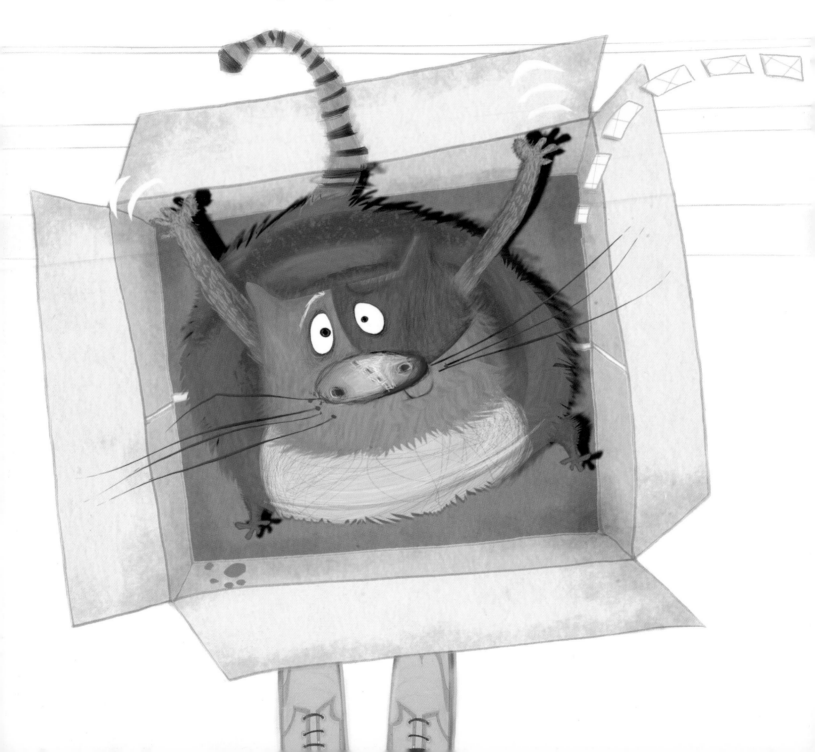

At first things weren't so bad.
Cornelius liked the company.

But as days went on,
things got worse...

On Monday, the fat cat was too messy.

On Tuesday, the fat
cat was too lazy.

MOW
MOW
MEGOOW!

AG Gh!

HOWL

La La La!

On Wednesday, the fat
cat was too noisy.

On Thursday, the fat cat was too smelly.

scritch
scratch

DRAT THAT FAT CAT!

And on Friday, he was far too much of everything!

By Saturday, Cornelius had finally had

enough!

Then it was time
to clean up!

Cornelius felt better.
No mess.
No noise.
No stinky smells!

ah hhh!

But without the mess and the noise—and even the stinky smells—Cornelius felt like there was something missing.

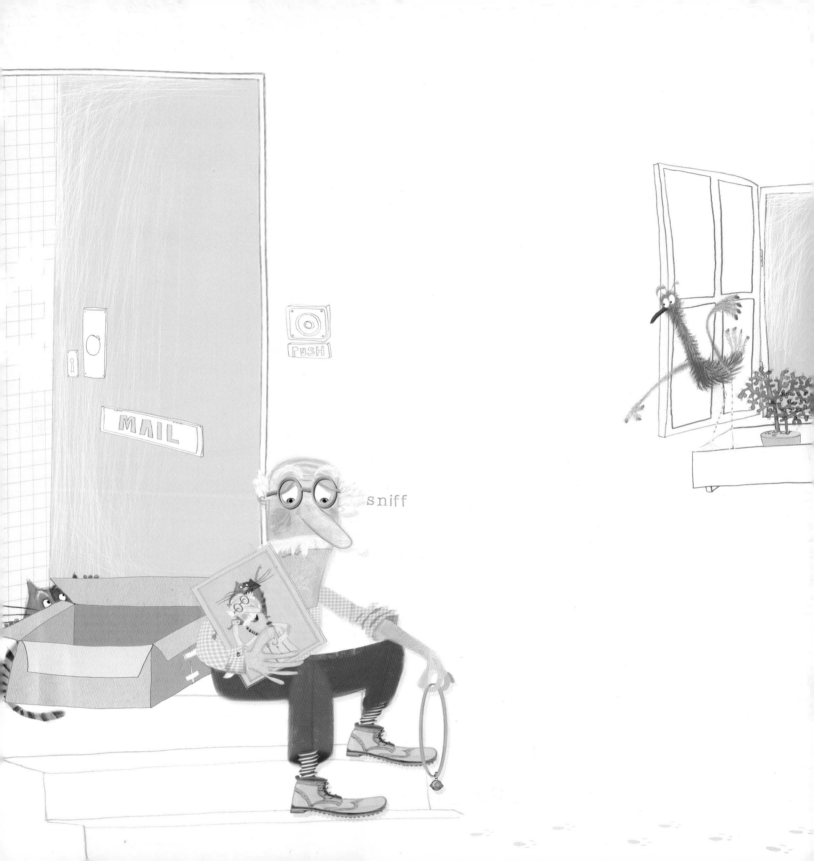

sniff

BRAT THAT FAT CAT!

So Cornelius searched
for that fat cat.

He looked high

and low.

He even dreamed of the fat cat that night.

And in the morning...

Cornelius found his fat cat at last!
They were both rather surprised at how
happy they were to be back together.

The fat cat promised to be tidier,
and Cornelius promised to be more patient.

Things were finally
back to normal.

meeoow!

CACTI

SUCCULENTS

CATS

Then one Sunday morning, there was a loud

DING

DONG!

WOOF!

at the front door.

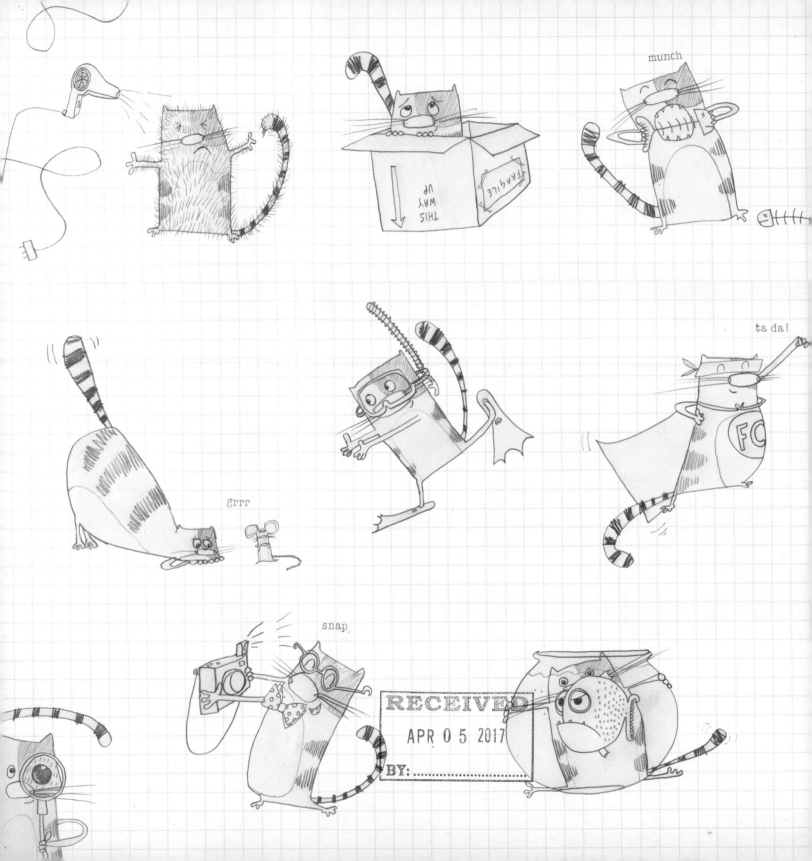